OPERATION ORANGUTAN

Dear Riley,
    The orangutans of Borneo need your help! Illegal logging is destroying their habitat and food sources. Join me, Aunt Martha and Cousin Alice in the Bornean rain forest to work with orangutan expert Dr. Cheryl Knott.
    We will be studying figs and fig wasps to learn why they are so important to the survival of orangutans and the rain forest. Time is running out, so I need you to go "ape" on this expedition!

Uncle Max

ADVENTURES OF RILEY
BY AMANDA LUMRY & LAURA HURWITZ

Eaglemont
Press

All photographs by Amanda Lumry except:
cover background, pg. 15 pygmy elephant, pg. 19 orangutan and pg. 21 paradise flying snake © Tim Laman/National Geographic Image Collection
pg. 5 river, pgs. 6-7 house and pgs. 22-23 camp © W. B. Karesh
pgs. 8-9 dipterocarp tree and pgs. 26-27 kuda kuda © Tim Laman
pg. 10 forest background, pg. 14 Sumatran rhino and pg. 25 forest trail © Harmony Frazier
pg. 13 sun bear and pgs. 30-31 orangutan © Nature Public Library
pg. 23 white-handed gibbon © Martin Harvey/NHPA

Illustrations and Layouts by Ulkutay & Ulkutay, London WC2E 9RZ
Editing and Digital Compositing by Michael E. Penman

Digital Imaging by Phoenix Color
Printed in China by Phoenix Asia
ISBN-10: 0-9748411-4-5
ISBN-13: 978-0-9748411-4-4

A special thanks to all the scientists who collaborated on this project. Your time and assistance are very much appreciated.

A portion of the proceeds from your purchase of this licensed product supports the stated educational mission of the Smithsonian Institution – "the increase and diffusion of knowledge." The name of the Smithsonian Institution and the sunburst logo are registered trademarks of the Smithsonian Institution and are registered in the U.S. Patent and Trademark Office.
www.si.edu

2% of the proceeds from this book will be donated to the Wildlife Conservation Society.
http://wcs.org

A royalty of approximately 1% of the estimated retail price of this book will be received by World Wildlife Fund (WWF). The Panda Device and WWF are registered trademarks. All rights reserved by World Wildlife Fund, Inc.
www.worldwildlife.org

First edition published 2007 by
Eaglemont Press
PMB 741
15600 NE 8th #B-1
Bellevue, WA 98008
1-877-590-9744
info@eaglemont.com
www.eaglemont.com

Library of Congress Cataloging-in-Publication Data

Lumry, Amanda.
  Operation orangutan / by Amanda Lumry & Laura Hurwitz.– 1st ed.
    p. cm. – (Adventures of Riley)
  Summary: While visiting his uncle in Borneo, nine-year-old Riley learns how illegal logging is endangering the rain forest and helps to rescue a baby orangutan.
  ISBN-13: 978-0-9748411-4-4 (hardcover : alk. paper)
  ISBN-10: 0-9748411-4-5 (hardcover : alk. paper)
 [1. Orangutan–Fiction. 2. Rain forests–Fiction. 3. Rain forest animals–Fiction. 4. Scientists–Fiction. 5. Borneo–Fiction] I. Hurwitz, Laura. II. Title.
  PZ7.L9787155Ope 2006
  [Fic]–dc22
                                        2006001847

"Pippen has been gone for days and I can't find him anywhere!" said Riley.
"But I have to go or I'll miss my flight."

"I'll keep looking for your cat while you're gone," said Riley's mother.

"Maybe you can find a cool new pet while we're in Borneo," said Alice.

Pippen was the best cat ever, thought Riley, but adopting a new pet from Borneo could be fun!

"Are we there yet?" Riley and Alice asked constantly as they traveled by plane, car and dugout canoe on their long trip to Borneo.

Borneo

➤ Borneo is the third largest island in the world, after Greenland and New Guinea.

➤ The rain forests of Borneo are the oldest in the world.

➤ Borneo is home to 210 types of mammals, 44 of which are found no where else in the world.

Dr. Marc Ancrenaz, Director, Kinabatangan Orangutan Conservation Project

Days later, a tired Uncle Max announced, "We're finally here!"
"Where exactly is here?" asked Alice.

"This is my rain forest home in Gunung Palung National Park! I'm Dr. Cheryl Knott, this is my daughter, Jessica, and this is my son ..."

Just then, a proboscis monkey leapt from a branch right in front of them.

"That's my son, Russell—the boy, not the monkey!" laughed Dr. Knott.

Alice elbowed Riley in the ribs. "Now, there's a pet for you."

Strangler Fig

▶ A strangler fig will wrap its roots around the tree it is growing on, which can strangle and kill the tree.

▶ A strangler fig usually begins life at the top of a tree and then grows down toward the ground.

▶ A strangler fig vine is a great place to watch for wildlife, since so many animals love to eat the figs!

Dr. Tim Laman,
Rain Forest Biologist,
Harvard University

Dr. Knott took them to a nearby tree with huge fig roots wrapped around it. Riley noticed a man high up in the branches.

"What's he doing?" he asked.

"That's my husband, Dr. Tim Laman," said Cheryl. "He's photographing orangutans while they eat figs. Dr. Laman uses ropes to climb the trees safely since they can grow as tall as a 15- story building!"

"What is so special about figs?" asked Alice.

"Figs are one of the only fruits that ripen throughout the year. Other local trees only fruit, or mast, every two to nine years. You'd get pretty hungry if you had to wait that long for your next meal! A fruit masting is a fantastic event to see, where large numbers of birds and other animals come together to feast," said Dr. Knott.

"I wish I could climb up there and see the orangutans up close," said Riley.

"Follow me!" said Aunt Martha.

Soon the whole group was soaring above the park in a special canopy raft, which hung below a small blimp piloted by Aunt Martha.

"Orangutans can be hard to spot," said Dr. Laman. "Look for moving branches or large nests made of twigs. You'll have a great view once we land on the treetops to collect fig and insect samples."

Fig Wasp

➤ Only a fig wasp can pollinate a fig. So, without fig wasps, there would be no figs!

➤ A fig wasp will let the wind carry it above the forest canopy.

➤ A fig wasp will use its sense of smell as a way to find ripe figs.

Erik Meijarrd, PhD.,
Senior Forest Ecologist,
The Nature Conservancy

"I'm hoping to learn why each species of fig is pollinated by its own type of fig wasp," said Uncle Max. "Why are fig wasps so picky and how do they know which fig species to pollinate? This has been a really tough problem for science to solve. Without fig wasps, figs couldn't produce any seeds and would eventually die out."

11

12 "Orangutan below!" shouted Alice.

Sun Bear

➤ The sun bear gets its name from the crescent-shaped, white or yellow mark often found on its chest.

➤ The sun bear is the smallest member of the bear family.

➤ The sun bear is an excellent tree climber and may build nests in trees to sleep or sunbathe.

Dr. Neal Woodman, Research Scientist and Curator of Mammals, National Museum of Natural History, Smithsonian Institution

Dr. Laman quickly zoomed in with his camera and saw, not an orangutan, but ...

"A sun bear!" said Dr. Knott. "Great spotting, Alice. What a rare sight!"

"Hey, Riley, how about that for a pet?" said Alice.

"Can you imagine the look on my mom's face if I brought home a bear?" asked Riley.

13

After returning to camp, Riley checked the hut carefully. "Uncle Max, these windows don't have any glass or screens. What will protect us from the elephants and Sumatran rhinos?"

"Actually," said Uncle Max, pulling out his field guide, "the local elephants, called pygmy elephants, can only be found on the northeast tip of the island. Sadly, the few rhinos that are left in Borneo might become extinct in twenty years."

Sumatran Rhino

- The Sumatran rhino is the smallest and hairiest of the species.
- Its front horn can grow up to 16 inches (40cm) in length.

Pygmy Elephant

- The pygmy elephant can grow up to 8 feet (2.4m) tall. That is only half as tall as a large African elephant.

- There are only about 1,600 pygmy elephants left in the world.

That night, Riley dreamed of searching Borneo to find the perfect pet.

16

In the morning they watched as Dr. Knott placed a plastic tarp under a nearby tree where a female orangutan was eating. In no time at all, the tarp was covered with ...

"Is that what I think it is?" asked Alice, wrinkling her nose.

Orangutan

➤ A male orangutan can weigh over 200 pounds (90kg).

➤ An orangutan will make a nest in the trees to sleep in. It will usually sleep in a different tree each night.

➤ An orangutan mother will use her body to form a bridge between two trees so that her baby can climb across.

Cheryl D. Knott, Ph.D., Associate Professor, Harvard University, Department of Anthropology

"It sure is," said Dr. Knott.

"Why do you collect orangutan pee?" asked Riley.

"I use urine, dung and hair samples to learn about the orangutan diet and life cycle. I'm trying to figure out why they give birth only once every eight years or so. That's the longest time between births of any mammal." Dr. Knott said.

"Collecting pee isn't for me," said Alice, "but orangutans sure seem more interesting than figs and wasps."

"They are all connected," said Uncle Max. "Figs are what orangutans eat when no other fruit is available. When mammals and birds eat figs, they spread the seeds onto the branches of surrounding trees. These seeds sprout into new fig vines, which means more figs for the future."

"So, without figs, orangutans would go extinct," said Riley.

"Probably not," said Dr. Laman, "but fewer figs would mean that fewer orangutans could survive the time between fruit mastings. That is one of the problems with illegal logging. It destroys the fig supply."

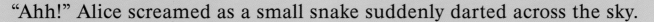

"Ahh!" Alice screamed as a small snake suddenly darted across the sky.

"We have flying frogs, too," said Russell.

"Now we're talking!" said Riley. "That would be a cool pet!"

Paradise Flying Snake

➤ It doesn't actually fly, but glides by flattening its body, leaping off of high branches and then slithering through the air in an S-shaped pattern.

➤ It may glide as far as 300 feet (100m) in a single leap.

➤ It can grow up to 4 feet (1.2m) long, and while venomous, it is harmless to humans.

Dr. Roy W. McDiarmid, Curator of Amphibians and Reptiles, National Museum of Natural History, Smithsonian Institution

Greater Naked Bat

➤ The naked bat is almost hairless!

➤ It has pouches along the sides of its body that it can push its wings into. This lets it walk around easier on all four limbs.

➤ It roosts in hollow trees, caves, buildings, rock crevices and holes in the earth.

Don E. Wilson,
Senior Scientist,
Smithsonian Institution

22

White-Handed Gibbon

➤ The bones of its hands are in a permanent hook shape so it can easily swing from tree to tree.

➤ At the age of six, a gibbon will leave its family to search for a mate.

➤ A gibbon's favorite food is fruit. It especially likes wild figs.

Margaret F. Kinnaird, Senior Conservation Ecologist, Wildlife Conservation Society

The next morning, loud cries from the gibbons woke Riley and Alice.

"Wake up!" Russell called. "Time to go exploring!"

Alice ran out wearing a helmet.

"What's that for?" asked Riley.

"I borrowed it from Dr. Laman. He uses it for protection while climbing trees," said Alice. "You never know what might land on your head around here."

"Like that bat we startled," said Russell, as one flew out the window.

23

As they walked along,
a flying frog whizzed by
Riley's head.
"Want to borrow
my helmet?" teased Alice.
"I'd rather follow that
frog ... this is my
chance
to catch
one!"
said
Riley.

Harlequin Tree Frog

➤ It doesn't really fly, but glides
by using the skin between its
fingers and toes as parachutes.

➤ It has sticky pads on the ends
of its fingers and toes to help it
grab the branch it glides to.

➤ It can glide up to
40 feet (12m) at a time.

*Jeremy F. Jacobs,
Museum Specialist,
Department of Vertebrate
Zoology, Smithsonian
Institution*

A shrill buzzing sound interrupted their frog chase.

"Is that a bird?" asked Alice.

She didn't see Russell motioning for her to be quiet or the ... ROOT.

"OUCH!" she screamed, flying head over heels.

Suddenly, the noise stopped.

"That wasn't a bird. That was a chain saw," Russell told them. "The loggers get closer every day. Your scream probably scared them off. Good job!"

"What are these train tracks for?" asked Riley.

"It's a kuda kuda," Russell told him. "Loggers use them to drag trees down to the river."

"And what is that?" Riley asked, pointing to a small wooden cage. A tiny animal huddled inside.
"Riley, your new pet!" said Alice.
"No," said Russell. "That is a wild baby orangutan. Look how scared he is! He must have lost his mother to the loggers. I've seen this happen before. Let's take him back to camp so that my mom can take care of him."

"What do we have here?" asked Dr. Knott as the group reached camp.

"We found him next to a kuda kuda," said Alice. "I think Riley wants to adopt him."

Riley blushed. She was right. "He may be cute now, but wait until he's an adult and weighs over two hundred pounds," said Aunt Martha.

"That's true," said Riley, "he's really not meant to be a pet for me, or anyone else. But can he survive without his mother?"

"He has a good chance," said Dr. Knott. "I know of a special camp where trained people can help him return to life in the forest."

With all the attention on the baby orangutan, nobody noticed how loud and busy the forest had become. Nobody, that is, except Alice.

"Mom, look at all the birds and animals. It looks like a family reunion!" said Alice. Creatures everywhere were flying, swinging and slithering into action. "The forest is having a fruit masting!" said Dr. Knott. They all took a moment to enjoy the sight.

Orangutan

➤ In the Malay language, *orangutan* means *man of the forest.*

➤ Sumatra and Borneo are the only places in the world to find a wild orangutan.

June Mary Rubis,
Researcher,
Wildlife Conservation
Society, Malaysia

31

Newly Discovered Mammal

➤ Announced in 2005, it is the first new carnivore to be discovered in Borneo since 1895.

➤ Slightly larger than a domestic cat, scientists don't know yet if it is a cat, dog, marten or fox.

➤ The only proof that it exists are two photographs from a camera trap.

Max "Uncle Max" Plimpton, Professor and Field Biologist

"I never dreamed we would see such a rare event," said Uncle Max.

"Borneo is so unpredictable," said Alice. "You never know what's going to happen next!"

"What you're looking for isn't always what you find," said Riley. "Isn't that what science is all about, Uncle Max?"

"Absolutely," he replied. "I was looking for fig wasps and found a fruit masting instead! I still have no clue why certain fig wasps are attracted to only certain figs, but our time here is almost over, so science will have to wait a little longer for the answer."

Dr. Knott added, "The rain forest is a giant puzzle that we are still trying to solve. That's why it is so important that we don't lose any of the pieces to logging or anything else."

"Whether it's fig wasps or orangutans, we need them all," said Riley.

Back home, Riley's mom had two furry surprises waiting for him!
She had found Pippen at the local animal shelter, where she had also
adopted a fluffy new calico kitten! Riley showed them his pictures of the
fruit masting, sun bear and orphan orangutan. He decided to name the
new cat "Fig" in honor of his trip. Riley returned to living the life
of a nine year old, until he once again heard from Uncle Max.

Where will Riley go next?

FURTHER INFORMATION

Glossary:

Dr. Cheryl Knott, and her husband, Dr. Tim Laman, are real scientists! They have both been working in an Indonesian National Park called Gunung Palung for more than ten years, and they really do have two children named Russell and Jessica.

There is a research station located there deep in the rain forest, where Cheryl, Tim and other Indonesian and Western scientists have been working trying to learn more about the plants and animals of the rain forest. This park is one of the most important places in the world for orangutans because it is one of just a few places where there is a population of over 1,000 orangutans left. That is why they are the special focus of Cheryl's research here.

There are problems with illegal logging in the park, but recently, the Indonesian government has made some real progress in stopping the logging and protecting this very important area. This is encouraging because, without these efforts, orangutans and all the other animals would have no place left to live.

AGILE: Quick and graceful.

CANOPY: The top layer of tree branches which cover a forest like a roof.

CREVICE: A narrow crack.

DOMESTIC: Local to a particular place or country.

FRUIT MASTING: When the fruit of trees in one area ripen at the same time.

ILLEGAL: Something that is against the law.

POLLINATE: To fertilize by carrying pollen to the female part of a plant.

REUNION: When separated members of a of a group gather together.

ROOST: A place on which a bird or other animal can sleep or rest.

UNPREDICTABLE: Not expected or known beforehand.

VENOMOUS: Having the ability to transmit poison by a sting or a bite.

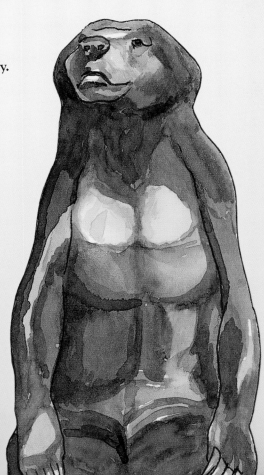